**A Fish Tale
By Dr. Rhythm**

From an idea by the Brothers Grimm

Dr. Rhythm is also known as Dr. B. L. Buddy Fish, an Associate Professor of Early Childhood Education at Jackson State University. He has been studying about Emotional Intelligence for over 15 years. His book for parents and teachers, *Raising Emotionally Intelligent Children: Introduction to Emotional Intelligence* is available at a bookstore near you.

You can also hear Dr. Rhythm tell this story on his children's album "You're Amazing!"

A note to parents and teachers: This book is about two imaginary people from the lower socio-economic strata. By our standards, they live in poverty. One of the characters, Herman, is happy with his lot in life; but Gertrude wants the "good life." Her happiness stems from what she can acquire in material goods—fancy foods, bigger houses, servants, power, etc. We see how Gertrude becomes greedier and greedier. The more she gets, the more she wants. Toward the end of the story, Herman tries to convince her to be grateful for all of the things she has gained from the magic fish; but she doesn't heed his words and suffers the consequences of her actions. It might just do us all some good to take a look at the consequences of our actions and how our feelings affect our thought and actions. We call this process consequential thinking. blf

Boys and girls, I want to tell you about a character trait known as GREED.

Greed is something that grows and grows inside of us.

We'll find out about it in this story about a magic fish.

We'll call it "A Fish Tale."

On an island, far, far away, off the coast of Vishnobia in the Veshtolobic Sea, lived an old couple-
Herman and Gertrude.

Herman was a fisherman. He spent his days fishing. He was as happy as he could be.

His wife Gertrude, though, was, oh, just a little bit greedy. She always wanted a little bit more than she had.

Well, one day Herman was out fishing. He threw out his line...

And lo and behold,
he caught a fish.

He reeled it in...

he reeled it...

and reeled it...

and there it was!

and the fish looked at Herman,

and Herman looked at the fish.

He'd never looked at a fish like that before, and

the fish said,

"Oh, Herman, please don't catch me. I'm a magic fish."

"And if you'll let me go, I'll grant you three wishes for your wife Gertrude, who I know *always wants more*."

"Well," Herman thought to himself, "how could that fish know about my wife Gertrude? He must be a magic fish."

So, he let the fish go...

and he went on home.

Gertrude was waiting for him.

"Herman, where's our fish? I'm ready to eat! I'm starving to death!"

"Oh, Gertrude, I found a magic fish, and the fish said he would grant us three wishes if I let him go. So, I let him go."

"Well, Herman, I don't know how you could be so gullible. You go back and you tell that fish that I want all the food that I can eat. I want my refrigerator full and my pantries full and everything!"

Herman went back to the water, and he thought for a minute and thought of a song:

"Oh, Fish in the sea,
Come and listen to me.
My wife begs a wish
From the magic fish."

The fish popped out of the water.

"Herman, it's good to see you, again."

"Well, Mr. Fish, you were right. My wife Gertrude wants all of the food we can eat, and she wants her refrigerator and pantries full. Is this too much?"

Herman went home, and there was all the food you could think of.

Gertrude was cooking,

and they were just as happy as they could be for about two weeks.

Then Gertrude looked at Herman and said,

"Herman, you go back and you tell that fish that I want to be Queen of this whole island!"

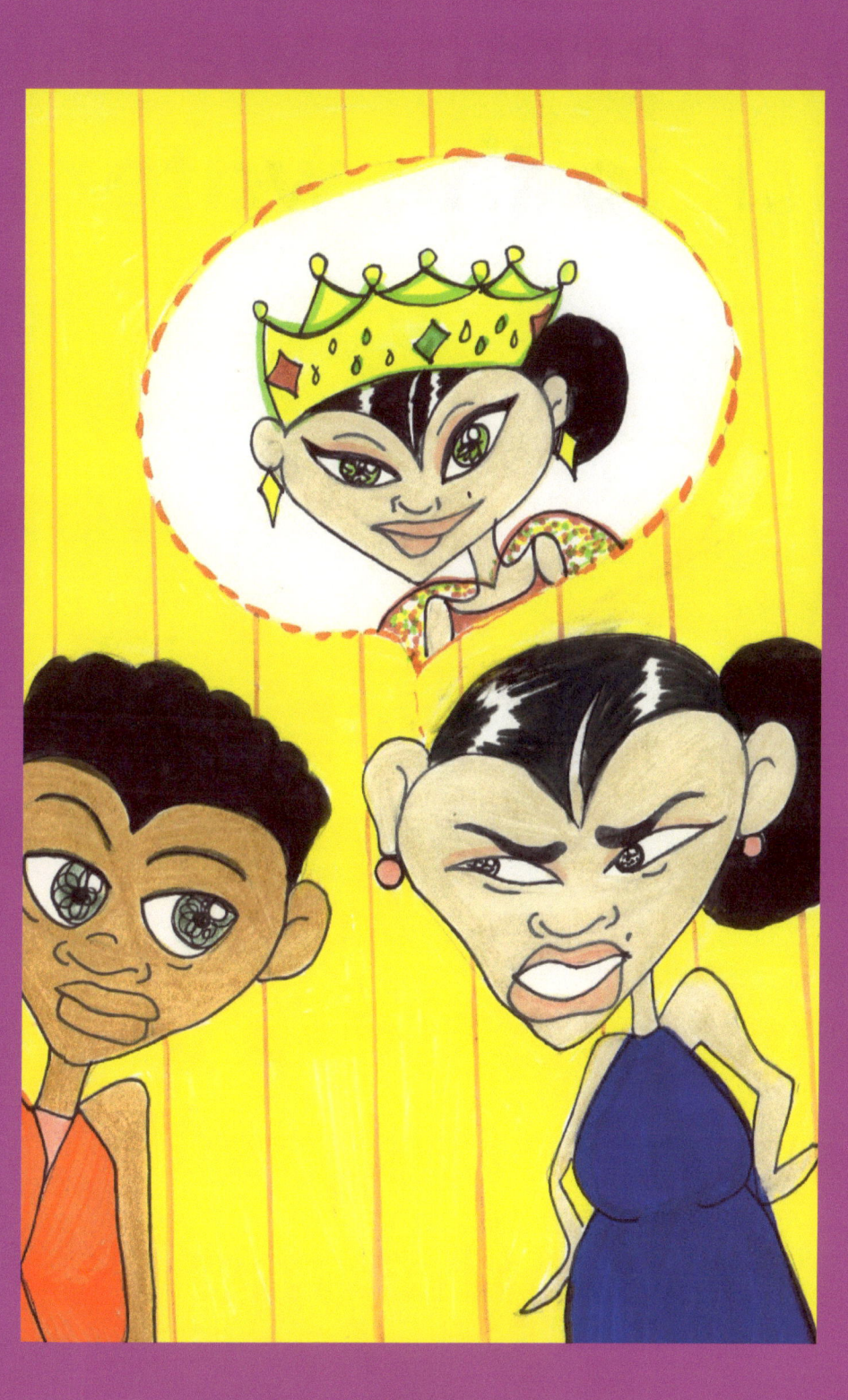

So, Herman went back to the water.

"Fish in the sea,
Come and listen to me.
My wife begs a wish
From the magic fish."

"Fish in the sea,
Come and listen to me.
My wife begs a wish
From the magic fish."

The fish popped out of the water.

"Herman, it's good to see you, again. What can I do for you?"

"Well, Gertrude...now, she wants to be Queen of the whole island. Can you do that for us?"

"I'll take care of you. You go back home and you see."

Herman went back home...

and there was a BIG castle,

and Gertrude was sitting on a throne.

And there were maids, and servants, and butlers running around.

And they had all the food they wanted and a big castle, and she was Queen of the island.

They were happy
for about a month...

and then Gertrude said, "Herman, you go back and tell that fish that I want to be Queen of not only the island, but the whole land of Vishnobia and everywhere around us!"

Herman went to the water.

"Oh, Fish in the sea,
Come and listen to me.
My wife begs a wish
From the magic fish."

Well, the fish came.

"Herman, how can I help you? I'd love to help you with your last wish."

"Well, she wants to be Queen of not only the land of the island, but the land of Vishnobia, too."

"O.K., I think that's your third wish, then Herman, not your second. You go back and you see."

Herman went back, and Gertrude was there. And she was Queen of the island and the land of Vishno- bia and all of the lands around,

and she was happy

for about two months.

Then Herman looked at Gertrude, and he said,

"Gertrude, isn't it wonderful to be Queen and King of the land?"

"Herman, you go back and you tell that fish that I want to be queen of the whole world and the earth, and the stars, and the sun, and the moon and everything!"

"But, Gertrude, we're...... shouldn't we be happy? We have everything we could want!"

"Herman, you go back and you tell that fish that's what I said, and I don't want any other answers from you!"

"Oh, Fish in the sea,
Come and listen to me.
My wife begs a wish
From the magic fish."

"Oh, Fish in the sea,
Come and listen to me.
My wife begs a wish
From the magic fish."

"Can you help me?"

"Oh, Fish in the sea,
Come and listen to me.
My wife begs a wish
From the magic fish."

"Oh, Fish in the sea..."

Well, the fish popped out of the water, and this time the fish wasn't so happy.

"Herman, you are too greedy. I'm going to take away everything that you've ever had."

Herman went back home and there was Gertrude, back in their little shack cooking the little fish they had left. She was too **greedy**.

Oh, Fish in the sea,
Come and listen to me.
My wife begs a wish
From the magic fish.

Oh, Fish in the sea,
Come and listen to me.
My wife begs a wish
From the magic fish...

The end,
Friend!